Blessings of Guadalupe

BLESSINGS OF
GUADALUPE

Text and Photographs by Eryk Hanut

Foreword by Tey Marianna Nunn, Ph.D.

Council Oak Books
San Francisco / Tulsa

For Nancy Steinbeck, holy and wild, my beloved sister

Council Oak Books, LLC
1290 Chestnut Street, Ste. 2, San Francisco, CA 94109
1615 S. Baltimore Avenue, Ste. 3, Tulsa, OK 74119

ISBN 1-57178-113-7
First edition / First printing.
Printed in South Korea.

02 03 04 05 06 07 5 4 3 2 1

And this is the way of Guadalupe:
Do listen to me, my littlest ones;
I want a shrine in your heart where I will reveal myself;
I will come down from above
And here I will reveal myself to you.

       —*Salve* (Anonymous, sixteenth century)

FOREWORD

When La Virgen de Guadalupe appeared to Juan Diego on the Hill of Tepeyac, little did she know what a sensation she would cause from that moment on. Or did she? Since her miraculous appearance in 1531, Nuestra Señora de Guadalupe, La Reina de las Americas, has become ubiquitous. She is an important religious and spiritual symbol for people from all walks of life. In Mexico, not only is she the focus of the largest pilgrimage site in the country, she has become a personal symbol for *Mexicanidad* or Mexican identity. As such she equals, if not supercedes, the red, white and green *bandera* (flag). This has become so evident that she is often depicted with a red gown and a green *manta* (cloak) in these *colores nacionales* (national colors).

Even the angel on whose outstretched hands she floats has wings in these Mexican colors.

La Lupe, or Lupita, as she is affectionately known, continues to play an important role in many lives. Her great influence is felt not only in Mexico but in much of Latin America and the United States as well. Both men and women are named after her, especially if they are born on her feast day, December 12. Writers incorporate aspects of this cultural icon in their work and artists, both conventionally schooled and self-taught, depict her in a variety of media. Her image appears on everything from the dinner plates in a restaurant named La Guadalupana to nail clippers, aerosol room freshener, and children's puzzles. Her name can be found on the placards of funeral homes, stores, towns, and churches.

Why is she so popular in Mexico, Latin America and beyond? It is because not only is she the mother of God, she is also human like us. These qualities make the connection to her deeply personal for each devotee. This wonderful little book,

Blessings of Guadalupe, helps to bring this personal side of Nuestra Señora de Guadalupe a little closer to all of us.

¡Que Viva Guadalupe!

¡Que Viva!

—Tey Marianna Nunn, Santa Fe, New Mexico

Al viajar de Júxtepec á San Francisco Sov...quitlam,
y seguir una vereda, se encabritó el jumento,..de
cayó peligrosa caída en la tierra del Subbey y á Sr.
Antonio Mendoza que creyó no aliviarse; pero el encomendar-
se á la Sma. Virgen de Guadalupe quedó sano.
A tan grande prodigio dedica el presente.

Pind Peñalva.

This is the story of the visit of Guadalupe, la Nuestra Señora de Guadalupe, to the small town of Santa Jacinta, which is near a bigger town, Juarez, which is near another bigger town, Chihuahua. It happened a long time ago, when donkeys were walking down the only street of Santa Jacinta, when you could still see shepherd's dogs chasing lambs in the fields, when there was no television or telephone, and when the only clouds of smoke hovering above the village were coming from wood fires in the fall, and not from factories.

This is a true story that unfolded in just one miraculous afternoon, a true story I was told by my grandfather when I was still a child.

And now my time has come to tell it to you—the great story of how Nuestra Señora de Guadalupe, our Mother and our Queen, brought smiles where there were tears and joy where there was grief, and health where there was suffering and disease.

And this is how it all began.

Knock, knock, knock.

Old Epífano couldn't get out of bed. With a cough, he yelled, "Come in," wondering who was knocking at his door. Nobody ever did, perhaps because he yelled all the time.

Nuestra Señora de Guadalupe entered the small dingy room that had no pictures nor flowers and reeked of old medicines. As she swept in, even the old tiles she was standing on glittered like pure gold, and the light pouring through the only window sparkled like emeralds on a bracelet.

"Why did you turn the light on, woman?" Epífano said, his eyes closed to the heavenly light that was emanating from his visitor. "Power is expensive! There is always enough light for me to see the color of my thoughts!"

Hallándose muy malo de dolor de costado D[on] Franco Schumann con mucha Fe se encomendó a N[uestra] S[eñora] de Guadalupe y luego se restableció y en agradecimiento de tanto beneficio le dedica este retablo. Mayo 20 d[e] 1891.

Nuestra Señora de Guadalupe sat on the bed, smiling.

"And why did you perfume yourself so heavily, woman? What do you want from me? I have no health nor money for creatures like you, you should know better!"

"I have come to bring you joy, Epífano."

"I told you, woman, that I don't have any money for the joy you might bring." Nuestra Señora de Guadalupe lifted her head and pointed at a glass of water at his bedside. The water started to spin out and out of the tiny maelstrom, images began to dance, as in a snow globe. Epífano's life started to unravel before him. At first, he saw himself as a boy, sitting by the river with his mother. Then, Epífano watched himself getting married to the lovely Lucita. What a happy day it had been, and how beautiful his bride was. Then he witnessed the arrival of his four children, each one of them a blessing.

Then the water seemed to turn darker, and other images emerged: Epífano working late, staggering home, drunk. Endless scenes with Lucita and her crying, late at night. Lucita had gone long ago now, and his children were too busy with their lives in big cities to see him. The final image was that of a bitter old man sitting in his bed with his head in his hands.

The water that seemed to be lit from the inside stopped swirling. Epífano knelt: "My owner and my Queen, I am so sorry for the pain I have caused. I am so sad for all that I have missed."

Nuestra Señora de Guadalupe touched his head: "It is never too late, my most cherished son—never too late to open your heart to me. It is up to you to establish the happy earth, because I gave you a vision of Glory. Therefore, lift up your head. Glory be to your Mother! Drink from my torrent!"

Again the glass of water turned into a magic lantern and Epífano saw himself, at the age he was now, in his very own house, but the house was filled with laughter and light, and he was surrounded by his whole family.

The old man prostrated himself in tears before the Queen of Heaven and Earth. Tenderly the Virgin said: "Be happy for what you have. Keep your heart open to me and you will never be alone."

Nuestra Señora de Guadalupe left the room, leaving behind her a happy old man and a strong perfume of wild roses that lasted for weeks.

Knock, knock, knock.

"**C**ome in!" answered Armanda. Armanda was young and beautiful. And very unhappy.

"Ah, there you are! It is about time, really!" she pouted, not at all amazed at recognizing the face generations had prayed to. "I've been asking your help forever!"

"I know," replied the Mother, sitting at the kitchen table next to her. "That is why I came."

"So, what are you going do for me?" asked Armanda defiantly, rising to her feet, her hands on her hips. "I need another job, a job that pays well, a job that won't ruin my hands. And I am tired of lousy boyfriends. I want a good husband—a rich one!"

Hallandose Gravemente mala la Sª Dª Tereza Sª Mª y en
el trascurso de 5 meses: no se sabia su enfermedad y a N. Sª
Maria Santisima de Guadalupe se dedicó cual era su
enfermedad y en justo Reconocimiento dedica este á 12
de octubre de
1855.

The Mother of Heaven and Earth smiled and took Armanda's hand in hers: "I will give you just enough," she whispered.

"Just enough?" Armanda sounded puzzled.

"Yes. I will give you enough sun to keep your heart bright
And enough rain so you always love the sun.
I will give you enough happiness to keep your spirit alive
And enough struggles so you will always cherish the small joys in life.
And, don't worry, I will give you enough money to satisfy your desires,
And just enough loss so you bless all you possess."

The Virgin's voice was so gentle that Armanda's eyes filled with tears: "How could I have been so wrong for so long, Madre?"

"Don't say you were wrong, you've just been lost in a fog. Think of the early spring days here, when the sun heats up the ponds around the village, and warm mist pours down the street and makes people stumble like blind men. You were not wrong, you were just seeking for direction and now you have found it."

The Mother closed her eyes and her right hand and seemed to be praying. Then she opened both. In her palm lay a thin gold chain with a perfect heart-shaped diamond at the end of it.

"This is for you, my most cherished daughter. Wear this under your clothes, where no one but you can see it. And when you feel lost, just touch it and you will taste my essence; each time you feel bewildered or don't know what to do or where to turn, remember the grace I bring you from Heaven."

Knock, knock, knock.

"Go away! Come back later!" yelled Diego the sacristan, who prided himself on being the village priest's right hand. He was counting piles of banknotes, pilling them in five-, ten- and twenty-peso stacks, and he didn't want to be bothered now!

When he heard a second knock, he lost his temper.

"I told you to come back later!!" he shouted. "Can't you leave honest people working in peace?"

The door swung open and the Blessed Mother of Guadalupe entered, ringed by light. This time, however, the light had changed from golden to dark blue, a shiny lapis color. And this time, she wasn't smiling.

"I am not selling candles right now! Nor flowers!!" growled Diego without raising his head. "Go to the church. They must have some left there. Come back tomorrow if you want something fancy."

Guadalupe slapped her hand down on the desk and said sternly:

"Diego, you have to change your life."

"Huh?!" The old man jumped, astonished at what he saw—a tall woman whose feet didn't touch the ground and who was emanating dark blue light.

"Look." She pointed, and Diego saw that the banknotes he had been so carefully protecting from the eyes of his visitor had turned into maggots—fat, juicy maggots.

"Take your curse back, Diablera, Evil Witch!! Take everything I have! But go now!! Leave with your curse!" Now the old man was really terrified.

The Virgin went on, her voice strong and a little threatening:

"Remember, Diego, all the presents, those little cheap things your wife so wanted and that you always refused her? Remember that little glass-bead bracelet? All these little joys you forbade her and now, you even steal money from the poor! I've seen you! Your candles are so expensive—and you even sell the ones the factory sent you without wicks. And the flowers!! Those flowers you sell for my altar are all faded. You sprinkle them with some vinegar to make them look fresher, but they die in minutes at my feet. It grieves me to see my once innocent child destroyed because of greed. Think of all the joy the money you get could bring. Think of all the people that could be helped with that money."

Diego the sacristan wanted to run away but two vines, rubbery and leafless like two licorice twists, had sprung from the banknotes. The two vines were chaining him to his desk. Diego started to twist and moan.

"I am not done with you yet, Diego."

Pedro Reyes inando que su esposa Señora Vicenta
... te dedicara a la Virgen de Guadalupe y ...

"Yes, yes, I'll do anything you want. I will, I promise!"

The poor man was near collapse. He now knew that he was in the presence of the Divine Mother. And he also knew that he had committed many sins.

"I've seen you," the Virgin said, "kicking the poor out of the church because they cannot afford candles, and these offerings you keep for yourself!"

"Please, forgive me. I won't be like that ever again. I want to change!" Tears started to fall down Diego's cheeks. At last, he was truly sorry.

The light around the Virgin turned from that blue color that clouds have in thunderstorms to the most dazzling gold. The vines that were keeping him prisoner turned into yellow petals.

"Diego, because you really want to change, I promise you that all your needs will be met. But from now on, the only gold that should matter to you is the gold of my Sacred Heart. Stop worrying about any other kind of riches."

Nuestra Señora de Guadalupe took Diego's head between her two hands:

> "My light surrounds you,
> My love surrounds you
> My power protects you
> My presence watches over you.
> Wherever you are, I am.
> Confidence in me will save you."

Diego very slowly got up from his chair and knelt before La Señora. "I wasted my life," he said, his shoulders shaking, "But now, I can begin again."

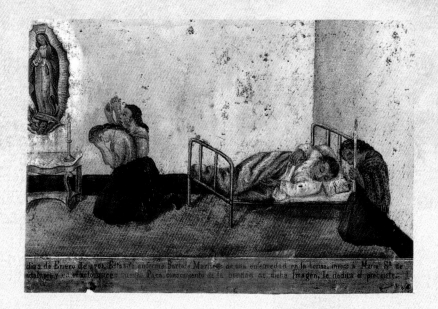

dias de Enero de 1901. Estando enfermo Bartolo Martinez de una enfermedad en la hernia, invocó á Maria S.ª de Acatzingo, y en el acto quedó bueno. Para conocimiento de la bondad de dicha Imagen, le dedica el presente.

Knock, knock, knock.

ittle Ignacio's mother had gone out and he felt too weak to get up and open the door. For months, very expensive doctors from as far as Chihuahua had come and gone at his bedside. They left bewildered. The little boy didn't show signs of any particular disease. He was just very weak and very sad. All the most fashionable medicines were piling up on his night table, next to less conventional fragrant remedies that Ignacio's mother had bought from a *curandera* in the mountains.

Some of the doctors had told his mother that the mysterious illness would disappear when "he would become a man." An old lady, wrinkled as an apple, had come from the deep country. She had burned small stacks of sage around his bed, assuring his parents that the sickness had been transferred to a tree, but Ignacio still lay sick in his bed.

The Virgin of Guadalupe entered the room. From the floor she picked up a blue ball that Ignacio had dropped weeks before and not bothered to pick up.

The Virgin sat on the little boy's bed, rolling the ball slowly between her palm and the pink bedsheet.

"You know who I am, don't you?" she said, softly.

"Yes," said Ignacio. "I saw you at the church, and I saw your portrait many times on people's walls."

"Why are you in bed?"

"I don't know. I never go out. I tire very easily. I don't have any friends. They just think I cannot run fast enough. They never ask me to play. I am tired of being sick, I am tired of being weak, I am tired of being tired."

NTRA SRA DE GUADALUPE

Nuestra Señora de Guadalupe, Our Mother and Our Queen, raised her right hand and the light that was surrounding her fell on Ignacio's body and then expanded to fill the whole room.

"A great happiness has risen, Ignacio.
Don't fear anymore.
Am I not also your mother?
Aren't you under my mantle of protection?
I will lift your suffering.
I am the Mother of all who live united in this land.
Always reach out to me
And from now on, love will spring.
Am I not also your mother?
Is there anything else you need?"

LA MADONNA SS. DI GUADALUPE

And that very day, the whole village saw Ignacio running out into the street, shouting with joy, his ivory complexion turned pink and glowing.

Quickly the news of La Guadalupe's visit spread through the village, and everyone heard about all the blessings that had been poured over the ochre roofs of its houses.

Santa Jacinta still stands today, another small village in the shadow of a bigger city. The miracles were too beautiful to be ever acknowledged by any Monsignor. The Clergy paid little attention to a hamlet of illiterate peasants: everyone knew, after all, they were so superstitious.

All the people who received the visit of Nuestra Señora de Guadalupe are long gone now. One by one, they died, happy and forever transformed.

Ignacio, my grandfather, was the last one to die, two years ago. He was good as bread and strong as an oak, and he had a good life. I never saw him sick. His last days were filled with love, reminiscence, and honor: a granddaughter's graduation, a grandson's Spanish ballad whispered in his ear. Before he died, he called me to his bedside and told me to tell the world this story.

Wherever he went, he always carried a small, worn-out blue ball, the visible, earthly reminder of the Divine embrace that had graced him all his life. The little blue ball rests on my desk now, a treasured possession. Whenever I look at it, I know that Someone above me is whispering: "I will lift your suffering. Am I not also your mother? Is there anything else you need?"

AFTERWORD

On December 9, 1531, the Virgin of Guadalupe appeared to a recently converted Aztec named Juan Diego on a hill in what is now the heart of Mexico City. She asked him to deliver a message to the Bishop: she wanted a shrine built there where she could welcome and bless all people. To prove that she was really appearing, she printed her image on Juan Diego's coat or *tilma*. Nearly five hundred years later, the image, printed on a material that normally doesn't last more than twenty years, is still fresh, and is venerated in the Basilica of Guadalupe in Mexico City.

For many all over the world, the phenomenon of Guadalupe is the greatest of all the Marian apparitions and prophetic of the Mother's birthing of a new world.

The photographs in this book are of paintings known as *retablos* (ex-votos) and folk art images of Guadalupe, given by pilgrims to the Basilica for graces received. All of them are now kept in the museum of the Basilica, located in a wing of the old baroque basilica (the new one opened on the same site in 1976).

Most of the lines that Guadalupe speaks in this story can be found in the original account of the apparition of 1531 and also in some Spanish-Latin "Salves" and devotional songs of the period.

May she bless us all.

—E.H.